Luke Was There

OTHER YEARLING BOOKS YOU WILL ENJOY:

MY BROTHER STEVIE, *Eleanor Clymer*
THE HORSE IN THE ATTIC, *Eleanor Clymer*
WE LIVED IN THE ALMONT, *Eleanor Clymer*
SANTIAGO'S SILVER MINE, *Eleanor Clymer*
THE SPIDER, THE CAVE AND THE POTTERY BOWL,
Eleanor Clymer
DEAR MR. HENSHAW, *Beverly Cleary*
HENRY HUGGINS, *Beverly Cleary*
COLUMBUS CIRCLE, *Patricia Reilly Giff*
RAT TEETH, *Patricia Reilly Giff*
THE WINTER WORM BUSINESS, *Patricia Reilly Giff*

YEARLING BOOKS/YOUNG YEARLINGS/YEARLING CLASSICS are designed especially to entertain and enlighten young people. Charles F. Reasoner, Professor Emeritus of Children's Literature and Reading, New York University, is consultant to this series.

For a complete listing of all Yearling titles, write to Dell Readers Service, P.O. Box 1045, South Holland, IL 60473.

Luke Was There

ELEANOR CLYMER

A Yearling Book

Published by
Dell Publishing
a division of
The Bantam Doubleday Dell Publishing Group, Inc.
666 Fifth Avenue
New York, New York 10103

ISBN: 0-440-40139-9

Printed in the United States of America

February 1989

10 9 8 7 6 5 4 3 2 1

CW

ONE

❧❧❧

You know how it is when you're a kid, and you think somebody is going to be there to take care of you, and then they aren't? First you feel scared. Then you get mad. Then you don't believe what anybody says. That's what this is about.

It's also about what happened last spring when we went to stay at the Children's House, Danny and me. My name is Julius. Danny is my brother. We had to go because my mother was sick.

But I have to start way back before that, when I was small, smaller than Danny is now. That was when my father and mother and me all lived together.

I sometimes try to remember the things that happened then so I won't forget them.

Like, I used to remember every year of my life from the time I was four. That was the year my father took me someplace, maybe it was a park, and put me on a horse. I was scared, because I was up so high and the horse was so big. But my father held on to me and pretty soon I liked it, and didn't want to get off. I can even remember the smell of the horse, though I can't remember where it was.

Then the next year, or maybe the year after, my father got me roller skates. I tried to skate and fell down, and the other kids laughed at me, and I cried. I guess I was five or six. But my father made me do it some more. He held me up till I could skate real good. I really felt happy. I felt like I could be sure he would take care of me.

He and my mother used to have arguments and yell at each other. I didn't like it, but I got kind of used to it. But one day he went away.

Before he went, he said to me, Julius, I have to go on a trip, but I'll be back and bring you a nice present.

I didn't want him to go, and I said, Don't go.

He said he had to, but not to worry, he'd

2

come back. Only he didn't. He never came back. I asked my mother where he was and she said, I don't know.

So there were the two of us. Then we moved in with my uncle. Most of the time he was out. Mama did the cooking and that. When my uncle was home he was all right, only he was always asking me, Julius, were you a good boy? What did you do in school?

When I told him, he would ask me all over again, especially if he was drinking beer. So after a while I quit telling him. Then he'd say, Can't you answer a question?

Sometimes he got mad at me, so I was a little scared of him. But at least he was there most of the time, at night anyhow. I always felt better when I heard him come in at night.

Then he left. He got married, and went to live somewhere else.

And then my mother got married to this man. His name was José. I liked him. He played with me. We'd go out in the street and play ball, and in the house he'd tease me, but I didn't mind because he would never do anything mean. He and Mama liked each other a lot. They went to the beach, or went fishing, and took me along. We had fun.

3

Then Mama had Danny. After that it was different, I don't know why. Danny lay in his crib and yelled, and Mama lay on the bed and just got up to cook supper when José came home. Then sometimes José wouldn't come home for a while, and when he did come home they had arguments. Like, Mama would say, Where were you? And he would say, Never mind.

I would go out and play in the street, or if it was raining I'd stay in the hall, because I didn't like it in the house, Danny crying and Mama and José arguing.

I'd say to José sometimes, Hey, man, let's go out and catch a few. And he'd say, Not now.

Then he left. I really felt bad then. And I guess Mama did too. After that we lived in different places, and sometimes she was home and sometimes she worked. When she worked, she would leave Danny at the day care place, and I would go there after school. But mostly she was home. I liked that better.

But then she got sick. That was in the winter. She took medicine and stayed in the house, and I would go to the store for her. She took care of Danny, and sometimes the neighbors would bring things they cooked, and one lady used to take Danny down to her apartment so Mama could sleep.

Mama didn't tell me what was the matter with her, and I wished she would get better. But I guess I got so used to it I didn't pay much attention, till one day when I got home from school, a doctor was there, a lady doctor. She was arguing with Mama.

She was saying Mama had to go to the hospital. Mama said she couldn't go. Who would take care of the children?

Then I began to get very scared. I said, No, no, don't go! Because if she went away who would be left?

But this lady doctor said, Don't worry, the children will go to a shelter. They will be well taken care of. I'll see to it myself.

So Mama said, Okay, if you're sure it's a good place. So the doctor phoned, and the ambulance came and took Mama away. Before she went she said, Be good boys and I'll be back very soon.

The neighbor took me and Danny to her apartment, and gave Danny ice cream to keep him quiet. Then after a while a lady came and took us both in a taxi, a long way away from our neighborhood. And that's how we came to the Children's House.

There were lots of kids, boys and girls, all ages. Danny cried, so the lady gave him candy and hugged him, and some big girls played with him. They put him to bed, and at first he was all right. But he woke up in the middle of the night and yelled, and I had to take him in my bed. He was scared because he didn't know where he was and Mama wasn't there.

I was scared too. In the daytime it wasn't so bad, because I thought, We just have to wait till Mama gets well, then we'll go home. But at night I had real scary thoughts. I got the idea, What if she doesn't get well? Suppose she dies!

Then I couldn't sleep. I felt cold all over, even with Danny in bed with me.

Well, a few days passed, and we went to school. It was a different school of course, but schools are schools. They're all the same. After school we went back to the Children's House and they let us watch TV or do things. Activities, like checkers, or reading.

I waited and waited, but nothing happened. I thought, Are we just going to stay here? How long?

6

Nobody was mean to us, we had food and clothes, but it was like we didn't belong to anybody. I wanted to find out about things, but I didn't know who would tell me. Mrs. Kronkite was the head of the place, but she was pretty strict and I didn't want to ask her anything. I asked Mrs. Randal. She was the housemother.

But she just said, Now, Julius, don't worry. Your mother will be all right soon, and meanwhile we want you to be happy here.

I said, Can't I go to see her?

She said, No, children can't go to hospitals to visit.

But they let me telephone.

When I finally got Mama on the phone, it didn't sound like her at all. She sounded far away, and she just said, Don't worry about me, Julius, I'm going to be all right very soon. How is Danny?

I said, Danny is all right. He's playing with some kids.

Then she said, How are you? Are you going to school? Do they treat you all right?

And I said yes, and then we said good-bye.

I didn't know any more than before.

Then I thought that if I could see the neighbors, they would know something. So one day after school, I went back to our neighborhood. I had no money so I went under the turnstile in the subway. I went to our apartment. I still had the key.

It was just the way we left it. After all, we were only away about a week, though it seemed like more. There were dishes on the table, some clothes on the bed, Danny's toys on the floor. I shivered. It wasn't cold, but I felt cold. I turned on the TV because I wanted to hear a noise. I looked in the refrigerator and found a Coke, so I sat down and drank it. I made believe Mama was out some place and would come in soon.

Then I heard a banging on the door. I yelled, Who's there?

The door opened. It was the super and our neighbor from downstairs. The super called out, Who's in there?

I said, It's me.

He said, Oh, it's the kid.

The neighbor said, Julius! What are you doing here? I heard the noise and I thought somebody had broken in so I called the super.

I said, I just wanted to see what's what. You heard from my mother?

She said she had been to see Mama and she was still sick.

I asked, When is she going to get better?

She said, She is getting better all the time.

I said, Nobody tells me anything about her. I just talked to her once on the phone.

The super said, Well, I have to go now, and you better go on back, they'll worry about you. Suppose you give me the key, in case you lose it. I'll take care of it.

I didn't want to give him the key, but when somebody tells you to do something like that, you sort of feel you have to do it.

I said, I want to take some of Danny's toys for him.

So the neighbor said, Okay, Super, I'll stay here with him.

The super went away. Then the neighbor said, Julius, I didn't know it was you, or I wouldn't have called him. You should have come to me first. How do they treat you down there?

I told her, All right, but I wish my mother would come home.

She said, Well, Julius, I didn't want to talk in front of the super, because I don't know how long she can keep the apartment. They said she has to have an operation, then she'll be all right.

I said, An operation!

That really shook me. I knew what that was from watching TV. But she said, Don't worry, she'll be okay. I wouldn't tell you that if I didn't mean it, believe me.

So I thought, Well, I better believe her.

I took some toys, a truck, and a bear that Danny used to go to bed with, and a couple of my things, and put them in a bag, and I went back to the subway.

When I got to the Children's House, Danny was crying. He had been looking for me. So I gave him his bear and his truck, and he was happy. But I felt terrible.

Well, after that I didn't much care what I did. I went to school but I didn't do any work. I just didn't care. I didn't even feel like eating. Mrs. Randal asked me if I felt all right. She said I needed vitamin pills and she gave me some, but they didn't do anything. I was just waiting. There was nothing else to do.

There was this other kid there, his name was Max. He was in my room in school, and he had the bed next to mine. I didn't like him much. He was always looking to see what

other people were doing, watching people.
He had ideas. He said we could swipe things
from the House and sell them, and then leave.
Maybe if it hadn't been for Danny I might
have done it, but I had a feeling that if Mama
didn't come back, I'd have to look out for
Danny. Anyhow, I just didn't care. I didn't
even want to watch TV.

I had this deck of cards that I brought from
home, and I had some comics. I used to play
cards with myself, and read the comics. I kept
the cards in my pocket and the comics under
my mattress. So when I came home from school
I'd lie on my bed and deal myself the cards,
and when I won three games I'd put them
away and read comics.

Well, one day when I was playing, this man
came in. He was black, real tall with glasses
and a black sweater. He stood there looking at
me and finally he said, Hi. You Julius?

I said, Yes, and he said, Well, my name is
Luke.

I asked him, Luke?

He said, Luke Morehouse. But you can call
me Luke.

I said, Okay. I didn't specially want to, but
I didn't feel like arguing.

So he told me, I'm your counselor.

I asked, What's that?

He said, It means an adviser. Anything you want me to advise you about, I will. If I can.

So I thought, Okay, advise me how I can get out of this place. (But I didn't say it out loud.)

He said, Come on in the living room with the rest of us. Not much fun staying by yourself.

I didn't want to, but I went. Might as well. I had found out that if you say no, you just get an argument, like, Oh, come on, don't be a grouch, we're all friends.

So I went.

TWO

❦❦❦

Max was there, and some other kids, and I could see they were waiting to see what this new guy would do, start a game, or ask us our names, or what?

But he just sat down. He had a book in his hand, and he was just starting to open it as if he was going to read, when a kid came and said that Mrs. Kronkite wanted to see him. He went out and left his coat hanging on a chair.

A couple of the kids thought they'd play some tricks. Max took his coat and tied knots in the sleeves, and one of the boys put ink in his book. The idea was, he'd get mad and yell at us, and then we'd do something else.

Well, he came back and picked up the book and said, You boys come over here.

I thought, Now we're going to get it.

He told us to sit down, then he started to read to us from the book. It was a pretty good book, all about a family that got shipwrecked on an island and had to find stuff to eat and a place to sleep. They were just going to sleep when they heard something growling in the bushes. It was getting real exciting when he stopped reading.

I asked, Well, what next?

He said, Ink.

There was ink all over about six pages so you couldn't see the words.

I said, Look what you guys did.

He asked me, Didn't you do anything?

I said, No.

Luke closed the book. One kid asked, Aren't you going to read any more?

He said, Well, I can't read this. Maybe I can find another copy somewhere. Right now it's time to wash for supper.

All evening I was wondering what happened to those people. Was it a lion? A wolf? It sure was dumb to put ink in the book. The next day Luke came back and he did have another copy of the book, and he read to us some more.

Well, after that things were better. I mean we had more to do. Luke came every day and we'd talk, or play games. He showed us how to do stunts—somersaults and handstands—and he even taught us boxing. Boy, that was fun.

Sometimes we went to the park and played ball. The first time we went, Luke said, Stay with me. Don't go too far away.

Some of us decided to fool him. When it was almost time to go back, we ran away and hid behind some big rocks. We heard Luke calling, Come on, kids, time to go home.

We didn't move. We thought he'd start looking for us, but he didn't. He blew a whistle. Then we came out, and he said, Look, you guys.

I thought he'd start yelling at us, but he didn't. He said, When I tell you to come, you come. Understand?

He wasn't fooling. He really meant it. So after that we did.

It's hard to explain, but Luke was different from the rest of the grownups around there. I mean, they were nice to us, but it was as if they had to stop and think how to talk to us, so we would take it the right way and not make trouble.

But Luke didn't have to stop and think, he just talked to us like we were people. For instance, some of the kids who were new wouldn't eat because the food was different from what they were used to. But Luke got them to eat. He didn't say, Just try this, it's delicious, just take a little. He just started eating himself and said, Not bad, see what you think.

After supper he helped us with our homework. I was glad because I always had trouble with math. He never said, You can do this if you just pay attention. Instead of that he'd say something like, Let's see if we can figure this one out.

I got used to having him around. In just a few days it seemed like he had always been at the House. I would run home from school because I knew he would be there.

One time when I walked in the door I heard this sound, Boom! Boom! Oom-bah, oom-bah! like a trumpet only very deep. I went up the stairs and it was getting louder and louder. I opened a door and there was Luke sitting with this big brass thing on his lap. It was like a trumpet only bigger than any trumpet you ever saw. He was blowing into it and this noise was coming out. Only it wasn't just a noise, he was playing music.

I guess I looked surprised because he stopped playing and laughed.

I said, What's that?

He said, It's a tuba. You never see one before?

I said, No, and he said, You want to try it?

I said, Me?

He said, Yeah. See if you have the lung power. Try it.

I took it on my lap and blew in the mouthpiece. Nothing happened.

He said, Harder! Give it all you've got!

I blew with all my might and the thing said, Boom!

He laughed again and said, Maybe I'll make a tuba player out of you. Get all these kids lined up and we'll have ourselves a band. How'd you like that?

I said, Great. How come you know how to do that?

He said, I used to play in a band. I wanted to be a band leader too, but I figured I could make better music right here. Come on, blow some more.

So I did, but I thought, What's the use? I could never get a big thing like a tuba.

But another time he had something that was real small. I saw him looking at his hand through a round piece of glass.

I asked him, What's that?

He said, Take a look.

And when I looked, it made his hand look bigger. The skin was like covered with lines, with hairs growing out of them! I asked, What kind of thing is that?

He said, It's a magnifying glass.

I looked at my fingernail. It was like a giant's fingernail, with dirt under it. I looked at my sleeve. The threads were like ropes.

I said, Hey, this is great! Then all the kids wanted to look. When Luke was saying good-night, I asked if I could see the glass again.

He said, All right, you can keep it for a few days. And he handed it to me. I had fun with that glass. I looked at everything through it. You could really see what things were. Like once I caught a bug in the park and looked at it, and I could see its little eyes and the hairs on its legs. And suddenly it opened its back and it had some wings underneath. I said, Hey, Luke! Look at this! It has four wings!

He said, Sure, it's an insect. Most all insects have four wings and six legs.

I said, What about a cockroach?

He said, Yep, most of them do too. Did you know that cockroaches have been around for 250 million years?

I said, No kidding! If they are that old maybe I better be nice to them instead of stepping on them. And he laughed as if I had really said something funny.

I wanted to know more about him, but I didn't want to be fresh. So one day I asked, Are you married?

He laughed and said, No, Julius, not yet.

So I asked him, Where do you live?

He said, I'll take you down there some time and show you.

So the next Saturday he took a few of us on a trip. There was me and Max and two other kids. We went on the bus, way downtown, and when we got off we walked quite a way. The streets were full of people, Puerto Rican and black, and some long-haired guys like hippies. And there were pushcarts with stuff on them.

Luke bought us some apples from a pushcart, and said, *Buenos días*, Carlos, to the man. And the man said, *Buenos días, amigo*!

Then he took us into a building, saying, This is where I live.

I was surprised. I thought he would live in some great place, but it looked poor, just an old house with dark stairs. But when we got inside his apartment it was different. It was all painted white. There was a bed with a yellow cover, and some chairs and a table, and a lot of books. It was on the top floor so it was real light.

I just stood there and stared all around. There was a rug, not on the floor, but hanging on the wall. It was yellow and gray and white and black.

Luke said, Sit down, kids, sit on the floor if you want. I didn't sit down, so he asked me, What's the matter, Julius, are you struck dumb?

I said, Gee, I like this place, and he said, I thought you would.

I asked him, Why have you got a rug on the wall?

He said, It's not to walk on, it's like a picture. An Indian woman made it.

I asked him, You know her?

He said, Yes. She lives out west in the desert. I'll show you a picture of her.

He showed us this picture of a woman in a

long purple skirt and a red blouse, standing in front of a little shack. There were two little kids in the picture, a boy with overalls on, and a girl with a long skirt like her mother's. And all around was just bare ground.

I wondered how they could live in a place like that.

Luke gave us Cokes and played some records, and after a while we started walking around looking at things. Max picked up a rock that looked like colored glass. I thought he was about to put it in his pocket. But Luke said, You know what that is? It's wood. Petrified wood. It used to be part of a tree, then it turned to stone about ten million years ago.

I looked at him to see if he was kidding but he meant it.

I asked, Where did you get it?

He said, In the desert. Some day you'll go there. It's beautiful.

I thought, Well, if he says so, maybe it is. I'd like to go with him.

But I didn't say anything out loud.

When we went back to the Children's House, I kept remembering the room with its bright colors and wishing I lived there too. I thought,

It would be nice to have a guy like that in your family. I think he liked me too.

Well, I was feeling pretty good. Then one day something happened. I was coming home from school, and I was excited because it was my birthday. I had almost forgotten about my birthday but that morning I got a letter. It was from my mother, only somebody else had addressed the envelope. Inside was a card, and a dollar, and she had written, Dear Julius, Have a happy birthday, buy yourself something and be a good boy and tell Danny to be good too. Love, Mama.

It was the first time I ever got a letter from my mother. She still didn't say when she was coming home, or when I could see her, but I thought, Hey! Luke is a counselor! This afternoon I'll ask him if he can find out.

So when I got to the House I went to look for him, but I couldn't find him. I went all over and asked the kids, but nobody had seen him. I asked Mrs. Randal.

She said, Oh, Luke is here. He's in the office talking to Mrs. Kronkite.

I didn't want to interrupt but I thought I'd stand near the door so I'd see him when he came out. The office door was shut. I could hear voices inside. Mrs. Kronkite's sounded mad, and Luke's was so low I could hardly hear him. I wondered what was happening. Was Mrs. Kronkite bawling him out? I thought she had some nerve if she was. Some of the boys saw me standing there and came over.

Just then the door opened and Luke and Mrs. Kronkite came out, still talking. I heard her say, The kids are more important than anything else.

Then she saw us and said, What do you want, boys? Shouldn't you be with your group?

I said, We're waiting for Luke.

Luke said, I was just going to look for you. Go to the living room and I'll be right there.

So we went, and pretty soon he came in. He said, Sit down, boys.

It seemed like that first day when he told us to sit down. That time we thought he would yell at us. This time we knew he wouldn't, but still I felt nervous.

Then he told us. He had to go away.

When I heard that, I felt as if a stone had hit me in the stomach. It was just like something that had happened before.

I asked, Where are you going? And he said,

I'm going to work in a hospital upstate, help take care of the patients. I have to go tomorrow.

I got up and started to walk away.

Luke said, Come here, Julius. I have something to say.

But I didn't want to listen. I didn't want to hear what he had to say. I walked across the room and stood by a window. The sun was shining, but the way I felt, it could have been dark. There was a jar with flowers on the window sill. I took it and threw it on the floor. Water spilled all around.

Mrs. Randal ran in and said, Julius! What's the matter with you?

I didn't even answer. I grabbed something else and threw it. A book, I think.

Then some kids started laughing, and somebody else threw something too. A bunch of grownups came in. They said, Stop that!

I yelled, I will not! I picked up a chair and threw it.

Then somebody grabbed me, and held on to me so I couldn't move. It was Luke. I didn't know he was so strong.

I thought, Now he'll be mad. I hope so, then I'll kick him. That'll be good for him.

But he wasn't mad. His face looked serious,

maybe sad, but not angry. He said, I know
how you feel, Julius. It's bad. It's real bad.
Let's talk.

So we went and sat down, me and Luke and
the other kids, and we talked. I didn't men-
tion my birthday, or my mother. At first I
didn't want to talk at all, but he kept needling
me, saying, Come on, Julius, what are you
mad at?

I said, I'm not mad.

He said, Yes you are.

I told him, Okay, I'm mad at you. You're
just like the rest. You make believe you like
us, then you go away. My father, my uncle,
José, you're all the same.

He asked, Who is José?

I told him, My stepfather. He went away
too.

Luke said, Maybe they didn't want to go. *I*
don't want to go.

Then I shouted at him, You're grown up
and you can do what you want. If you don't
want to go you don't have to.

He said, That's not so. Sometimes grownups have to do things they don't like.

Then he told us the reason. He was sup-
posed to go in the army, but he didn't want

to. He said he wouldn't shoot a gun or do anything that would kill people.

One kid asked, What if somebody tried to shoot you?

He answered, I'd try to get the gun away from him but I wouldn't shoot him.

Well, then they told him, Okay, don't go in the army, but you must put in time working to serve your country. You have to do something useful like work in a hospital for war veterans.

I asked him, Aren't you doing something useful here? Why can't you stay here?

Then he looked angry, real mad. He said, That's what I told them but they wouldn't listen. Mrs. Kronkite told them she needs me and you all need me more than the veterans do, but it's no use. (Then I understood why Mrs. Kronkite sounded mad. It made me like her a little better.)

Luke said, So I have to go away and work in this hospital, for a while anyhow. But I will be back if Mrs. Kronkite and I can make them change their minds. Do you believe me?

Some of the kids said, Yes, we believe you.

I didn't say anything. I couldn't talk.

Luke Was There

Luke put up his hand and made the peace sign, then he went away. Some of the kids cried. I felt like it but I didn't, not then. But after I was in bed I did.

That was some birthday.

THREE

The whole week after that I waited for Luke to come back. I thought he meant he was coming right away. I still had his magnifying glass, because he forgot to ask for it when he left. I kept it in my pocket and I would hold it in my hand there, or if nobody was around, I'd take it out and look through it. It made me feel a little better when I did that.

I thought about Luke coming back, and me saying, Here, Luke, you forgot this. Then he would say, You keep it, Julius, it's for you.

I went right home after school every day in case he was there.

Max wanted me to go with him, walk around the neighborhood and see what we could find. He asked me why I was in such a hurry to get back.

I said, I want to see if Luke is there.

Max said, Forget it, he's not coming.

I reminded him, He told us he would if he could.

But Max said, he hasn't showed up yet, has he? I bet they won't let him go. Those are the rules. They wouldn't change the rules for us.

I thought, Maybe he's right, them and their stupid rules. And I started getting mad again. I even felt mad at Luke.

So one day instead of going back to the House I went with Max. We walked around looking in the store windows. There was a bakery with some great-looking cakes in it.

Max said, I'm hungry, I think I'll get some of that cake.

I asked, How are you going to do that? Because I didn't think he had any money.

He said, Watch. And he went over to a lady and asked her, Missis, could you give me a quarter?

She looked surprised and asked, What for?

He said, I need to get home and I only have a dime. I lost the rest of my money.

I thought, What a nerve! I'd never be able to lie like that.

The lady looked as if she didn't believe it

either, but she gave him a quarter. After she went away, he went into the store and bought some doughnuts and we ate them, walking along the street.

After that I went out with Max after school every day. He knew all kinds of tricks. If he wanted candy or fruit he'd go inside the store and walk around touching things. The man would ask, What do you want, boys? Max would say, Nothing, we're just looking. The man couldn't watch us every minute, and when he looked away Max would grab something and stuff it in his pocket, and we'd leave.

There were some benches along the street, and sometimes a man or a lady would sit down to rest. Max had his eye on those benches.

I asked, What are you looking at?

He said, Just watch me and you'll see.

He watched till a lady put her pocketbook down on the bench. Then he grabbed it and started walking fast. We went around the corner and he took out the money. There was only about a dollar and some change. I looked back and the lady had jumped up and started yelling. She looked poor. I felt sorry for her. I was sure I'd never do a thing like that.

Max said, Come on, let's get away from here.

We went back to the House and Mrs. Randal asked, Where were you, boys?

Max said, The teacher wanted us to help her.

Mrs. Randal thought that was nice, so she didn't say any more.

Danny was standing by the door waiting for me, and he ran to me and said, Hi, Julius!

I felt bad about leaving him alone so much, but I said to myself, Oh, well, there are plenty of people here to take care of him.

I didn't feel too good about going with Max, either, but it was exciting, and I thought, He's my friend, and he wants me to come. And anyhow it's boring at the House.

One day Max said, Let's go to the supermarket.

We went in and saw a lady pushing a shopping cart, and her pocketbook was in the cart on top of the groceries. Max said, You stand by the door and run when I tell you.

Then he grabbed the pocketbook and came toward me. He stuck the pocketbook in my hand and said, Run!

I ran one way and he ran the other. But the

lady came out yelling, Stop those boys! A cop
was standing there and he grabbed Max. I
looked back from around a corner and saw it. I
thought, Max is smart, he'll think up a good
story. Then I saw he was pointing to me!

I thought, He's saying I stole the pocketbook!

I didn't know what to do except to run. So I
ran till I was out of breath. Then I stopped
and looked around.

Nobody was after me. I looked inside the
bag. There was just a wallet and a handker-
chief and some keys. I looked in the wallet—
there was no money, only some stamps. They
were food stamps, I knew because my mother
used to get them. I threw the whole thing
away.

Then I wondered what to do next. Suddenly
I thought, I can't go back to the House. The
cop will take Max back there and he'll say I
did it. That rat! I thought he was my friend.
Now I'll get arrested.

I began to feel real scared. I had never done
such a thing before.

I thought, Maybe they'll send me away. If
Luke was there, or my mother, they could
help me, but there wasn't anybody. I was all
alone.

I decided I might as well stay out. Of course Danny would cry, but he'd get over it.

It was getting late. I was hungry. But where could I get something to eat? I tried to think what Max would do. He'd swipe something. I went into a grocery store. It was busy in there, because people were coming home from work and buying their food. I took a package of cheese and some crackers and a cake and stuck them inside my shirt and walked out. I felt kind of scared and sick, doing that, but I didn't know what else to do.

I walked toward the park. The subway station was in that direction. I thought of going to our apartment. Then I remembered I didn't have the key, and even if I had it, the neighbors would see me and make me go back to the House.

The street lamps started to light up. I sat down on a bench. An old man was sitting there, and when the lights went on he started to read a newspaper. He held it up close to his eyes, as if he couldn't see too well.

I thought I'd try getting some money, and I asked him for a quarter. He shook his head no.

33

I said, Oh, come on, give me a quarter. A nickel.

The old man said, Sorry, sonny. I haven't got any money.

I reached in my shirt and took out the cheese and crackers and started to eat.

The old man asked me, Got any to spare?

I said, No. I was surprised at a grownup asking me for something.

He said, Oh, come on, you have plenty.

So I gave him some cheese and crackers. He gobbled them down.

I asked, What's the matter, didn't you eat today?

He said, No.

Then I asked him, Where do you live?

He said, I don't live anyplace. Where do you live?

I told him I didn't live anyplace either. It was a dumb thing to say. After all, I didn't know anything about him.

How come? he asked me. Kids have to live someplace.

I said, Not me.

He asked, Where you going to sleep?

I shook my head and he said, Come on. I'll show you something.

He got up and started into the park. I was scared, but I went with him. I thought, I can always run faster than he can.

The old man took me to a road in the park that was blocked off by logs. We climbed over the logs and walked till we came to a truck. It was in among the bushes, and it had no tires or lights or mirrors. But it still had a door and a roof.

I asked him, Is this yours?

He laughed and said, Mine? Nothing's mine. Sometimes I sleep here. You can too if you want. But don't tell anybody. I don't want a lot of drunks in here.

We climbed inside the truck. There were a lot of old newspapers in it. The old man said, I use those for blankets.

We lay down and covered ourselves with the newspapers. It was cold, and I was still hungry, but I fell asleep. I woke up a few times, because I was cold and hungry, but mainly because the old man snored. I listened to him for a while. Then I remembered that José used to snore. And my mother used to say, José, turn over. It seemed so long ago, it was something from another world. I gave the old man a push and said, Turn over. He rolled over and stopped snoring.

I tried to go back to sleep but I was cold. I put my hands in my pockets. The glass was in my right-hand pocket. I held it in my hand and wondered if Luke was back yet. At last I felt a little warmer, and went to sleep.

In the morning I was starved. I said to the old man, Mister, how do we get something to eat?

He said, Well, I found a place to sleep, how about you getting us some grub?

I didn't know how I would do it, but I climbed down and went over to the street where the stores were.

There was a bread truck in front of a store and a man got down with a basket full of bread. It smelled good. I thought of asking the man for some, but I was sure he would say no. What would Max do? I waited till the man was inside the store, then I tried to open the door of the truck. It was locked. Then I thought of going inside the store and grabbing something. Only I'd have to take enough for two, and I didn't think I could do it. Of course I could just leave the old man there—not go back. But that seemed like a mean thing to do. Later I was glad I didn't do it.

On the corner a lady was waiting for a bus. I

went over and asked her, Lady, give me a quarter?

She looked hard at me and asked, What for?

I said, I lost some of my carfare and I have to go to school.

She said, Boy, you look too dirty to go to school. Go home and wash and ask your mother for money.

I said, My mother's not home. (That was true, anyhow.)

She shook her head but she gave me a quarter. I ran to the store and said, Gimme a loaf of bread.

But the bread was 37 cents. The man said, Tell your mother to give you more money.

Now what should I do? I said, She told me to get bread for a quarter.

The man told me, Oh, maybe she meant for you to go to the half price store in the next block.

I ran there and found the store that sold day-old bread. I got a big loaf. Then I ran out and saw a milk truck and a man unloading boxes full of milk cartons. When he went into the store I grabbed a carton of milk and ran. The man came out yelling, Hey, you! But he didn't follow me.

I ran back to the park. A cop was standing by the entrance. I didn't want him to see me so I walked on and climbed over the wall and finally got to the truck.

The old man was sitting in the doorway reading one of the old newspapers. But he wasn't holding it up close to his eyes. He had my magnifying glass and was reading through it.

I thought, Now how did he get that? Did it fall out of my pocket?

I waited for him to say, Oh, here's your glass. But he only said, You sure took long enough. What you got?

I said, That's my glass you're reading with.

He said, What do you mean it's yours? I found it. Come on, let's see what you got for breakfast.

I said, First give me my glass. Or you won't get any food.

I was getting mad by this time. I guess he was hungry, because he threw the glass at me, and I caught it. Then I gave him some bread and we took turns drinking milk from the carton.

He started asking me where I was from. But I didn't answer. Then he told me he had two grandsons about my age, but he hadn't been to see them in a long time. They lived in the country, and had a pony. He said he bought it for them.

I thought it would be nice to have a grand-father, and maybe I could get to like this old guy and make believe he was my grandfather.

Then he asked me, No fooling, kid, where do you live?

So I told him, in the Bronx. I was just going to tell about the Children's House and that, when he said, They must be looking for you. I bet they're worried.

I said, No, they don't care.

He said, Well, let's go. And he climbed down and we walked toward the gate. I didn't see the cop at first. But when we got outside, there he was, just ahead of us. I said, Hey, there's a cop, let's go the other way.

But what did the old man do? He walked straight toward the cop. I heard him say, Offi-cer, this boy is lost. I found him wandering in the park.

I took one look at that old guy. Then I turned around and ran.

FOUR

I ran back into the park and ducked behind some bushes. Then I crawled farther away as quietly as I could. I heard the policeman and the old man tramping around and calling, Come on out, boy, we won't do anything to you.

But I didn't come out. I didn't believe them, especially the old man. The rat!

I thought, If I go back to the House, I'll go by myself, not with a cop.

At last they went away.

Then I had to decide what to do next. I had to get more food and a place to sleep. And I wanted to wash. I felt dirty from sleeping in the truck under the newspapers.

I walked through the park and found a building with a sign on it: MEN. I went in. You

40

could wash in there. You could even take a bath if you had a towel. I washed and dried with paper towels, and combed my hair with my fingers. But I guess I made too much noise, because a man came and asked me, Hey, kid, why aren't you in school?

School! That's all grownups think about.

I thought fast and said, My school is closed today.

He said, Oh! Okay.

I went out and walked around in the park. It was a nice spring day. The leaves were green and the whole park looked clean. For a while I felt real happy, not to be in the House or in school, just out by myself with nobody watching me. I wished it would last. But then I started to feel hungry, so I had to start worrying again about what to do.

I thought of the book Luke read to us, about the family that got shipwrecked and had to make it on their own. The only thing was, they had each other, and I was all alone. I wished I had somebody with me. It might have been fun.

Not far away I saw a lake. Near the lake, under some trees, a bunch of people were sitting—grown-up people but young. Just sitting on the grass. They had long hair and hippie clothes, and a couple of them were playing guitars. The rest were moving with the music, swaying, maybe humming a little. I went nearer.

They were eating, passing around sand-wiches, and a big plastic bag of vegetables—carrots and stuff. It made me hungry to watch them.

One guy saw me and called, Hey, kid!

I went closer. He held out the bag and said, Have some. So I sat down and they gave me food. The sandwiches were mostly peanut but-ter. They had a big bottle of some funny-looking stuff to drink. Tiger's milk, they called it. It tasted better than it looked.

We were sitting there minding our own busi-ness when a cop came along and said, Okay, get moving. No sitting on the grass.

Some of them argued with him and said, What's wrong, man? Lots of people are sitting on the grass.

But he wouldn't listen. He said, Come on, outa here.

So they got up and picked up their stuff and walked off. I went too because I didn't want the cop to notice me. I thought I'd go with them. But at the gate they just walked away. They didn't say good-by or anything. Just acted like they forgot about me. I stood there and watched them go.

Then I started to feel scared again—scared of being alone. I don't know what was the matter with me, why I didn't go back to the House. If I had gone back then, they would have yelled at me or even punished me. But, okay, you get punished and that's it. It wasn't that. It was more like, when you start going a certain way, you just can't stop. You can't turn around and go back unless something happens to make you.

I started walking along the street. I walked a long way, not thinking where I was going, except it was the opposite way from the Children's House. Suddenly I noticed some guys, teenagers, sitting on a stoop, and a few standing on the sidewalk.

I started to walk around them, and one said to me, Hey, where you going?

Like a dope I told them I was going to the store. So one of them said, Store, huh? You must have money.

I said, No, I haven't got any money.

They laughed. That's cool, going to the store

43

without money. And one of them grabbed me and started feeling my pockets. He didn't find any money but he found the magnifying glass.

I said, Leave that alone, that's mine.

He said, Oh, yeah? Maybe I can use it.

I suddenly got so mad I must have lost my mind. I yelled, You give me that! And I threw myself at him and tried to grab his hand.

He was a lot bigger than me and he could have fixed me good, but he was really only teasing me, holding his hand with the glass way up over my head. The others were laughing and one of them said, Come on, Mike, leave the kid alone.

So he said, Okay, go and get it, and he threw it in the middle of the street. The cars were going past and I thought, It's broken, I lost it. What'll I tell Luke? (As if I was going to see him again soon.)

But when the cars were gone I saw it lying there, and it wasn't broken. I picked it up and started running. I ran till I couldn't run any more, and I sat down on the sidewalk to rest. I thought, Well, I got away from them but what will happen next?

I was holding the glass in my hand and I started looking at things through it, first my

44

sleeve and then my hand, and then I looked at
the sidewalk. It was full of hills and valleys.

Then I noticed some feet near me. I looked
up, and there were some kids about my age,
looking down at me.

One of them asked, Hey, man, what you
doing?

I said, Oh, just sitting here.

He asked, What's that thing you have?

I said, Here, take a look. So he looked
through it and said, Wow! Everything is big!
Hey, guys, look at this!

They took turns looking. Then the first one
asked me, Where do you come from? You're
not from around here.

I told him, No, I live in the Bronx.

Then he asked, What are you doing on our
block?

I told them my mother was away, and I
came to see my aunt, and she wasn't home,
and I didn't have any money to get back. I
said, You have anything to eat?

The first one, his name was Louie, said,
You hungry?

I said yes. I wasn't really hungry yet, but I
knew I would be soon. So he said, Come up to
my house and I'll give you something. But I

didn't want to. I was afraid his mother would start asking me questions.

I asked him, Could you bring it down here?

He said he would. So he went away, and soon he was back with some sandwiches and bottles of Coke.

One of the other kids, his name was Fernando, said, Hey, let's go to our hideout.

But Louie said, You crazy? You want him to know about it?

Fernando said, Aw, it doesn't matter. He's from the Bronx.

So we went to this vacant building around the corner. The first floor windows and door were boarded up, but Fernando led the way around to the back, through an alley full of broken bottles and junk, to the cellar. From there we went up to an apartment. The door wasn't locked. It was dirty inside. There was broken plaster on the floor, and there was an old chair and a mattress. From the windows you could look down in the street.

Fernando said, Well, how do you like it?

I said, It's great. Hey, could I stay here?

Louie asked, Why do you want to stay here?

I told him, I'm not going home tonight. If my mother comes back I'll get a licking. I'm going to hide out for a few days till she cools off.

So they told me I could stay, and they would bring me some more food. Fernando said, You can sleep on the mattress, but don't stand too near the window, somebody might see you and call the cops.

I asked why, and he said, Because junkies come here.

I asked, What do I do if junkies come? He told me, Better hide. If you've got anything they'll take it off you.

We ate the sandwiches, and one of the kids had some cigarettes so we smoked a couple. Then they had to go, but they promised to come back later. After they left it was real quiet, and I sat there on the mattress waiting. I thought, I bet those kids don't come back.

I heard a scratching sound in a corner. It was a mouse. He found a piece of bread from one of the sandwiches, grabbed it and ran away. I wished he would come back. It was awful lonesome.

Now it was getting toward evening. I looked out of the window. I didn't think anyone would see me. The street lights were lit, and people were coming home from work. In a house across the street I saw a woman in a kitchen standing near the stove, cooking something. I began to feel real bad.

I thought, Why isn't my mother home cooking supper? Why doesn't she get well? Here I am in this dump, and she doesn't even know where I am. I thought, Maybe I should go back to the House. At least there are people there. And there's Danny. I wonder what he's doing.

Then I heard a noise on the stairs. Was it the junkies? I looked for a place to hide. I ran out in the hall and up the stairs. Then I heard voices.

It was the kids, and a man. The man said, Well, where is he? They were inside the apartment and the door was open.

Then I heard Louie's voice saying, Gee, Pop, I don't know. He was here, and he said he would stay.

I thought, What did Louie bring his father for? I didn't wait to find out. I ran down the stairs, out in the street, and into the next doorway that was open. This was a house that people lived in. I could smell food cooking. I felt so bad that I was almost crying. Just then a woman came in with some paper bags. She looked at me and asked, What's the matter?

I wanted to say, I have no place to live and nothing to eat, but I couldn't say that to a stranger. She would ask, Where's your mother? Why don't you go to a policeman?

She was waiting for me to answer, so I said, I had a dollar and some kids took it and I can't go to the store. . . .

She said, Wait a minute. And she reached in her pocketbook and gave me a dollar.

I was so surprised I didn't know what to do. She didn't look rich, just a woman coming home from work with bundles. I felt ashamed of lying to her. Didn't she know I was lying?

She asked me, Well, what do you say?

I said, Thanks, lady. I didn't think you'd do that.

She said, Once in a while we have to trust people. Now go home.

She went on up the stairs, and I looked out in the street. The kids were coming out of the empty house with a man. I hid till they were gone, then I started walking again.

FIVE

I didn't know where I was going. I was just walking. I stopped in a store and bought some pizza, and walked along eating it. I was getting awfully tired. What I wanted more than anything was to sleep in a bed. When I came to a subway station I had an idea. I went down and got on a train. I rode uptown and got off at my own stop.

It was real dark when I came out on the street, and nobody noticed me. I walked to my apartment house and looked up. Our windows were dark. I wished I had the key.

I walked through the alley and around to the back of the house. There used to be a way to get on the fire escape from the outside. We had an old ladder. You had to stand on the top

50

of it and you could reach the fire escape ladder. But it was gone.

I went back to the street and went in through the next building. Then I ran up to the roof and over to our building. I climbed down the fire escape till I got to our apartment, and looked in the bedroom window.

It was dark but I could see that our furniture was still there, the beds and dresser. So that meant my mother was still keeping the apartment.

I wanted to get in but the window was locked. I couldn't stand it. I got so mad sitting there on the fire escape and looking in at my own house that I got desperate. I took off my shoe and banged it on the window, right under the lock. I broke a hole in the glass. It didn't smash the whole glass. I sat there in the dark waiting to see if anybody had heard, but nobody came.

After maybe half an hour, I reached my hand in and unlocked the window and pushed it up. Then I crawled in.

I sat there in the bedroom, catching my breath, for another half hour. I thought, If anybody comes, I'll get to the fire escape and up to the roof. But nobody came. So I took off my other shoe and went to the kitchen. I was afraid to turn on a light, but I could see a little. I opened the refrigerator. There were some bottles of beer. That was about all.

I opened a closet and found a can of something. Beans. Okay, I could eat beans. I found the can opener and opened it. All the time I was trying not to make a sound. I got a spoon and ate the beans. I was thirsty so I drank some water.

After that I thought, Gee, I'd like to take a bath. But I was afraid if somebody heard the water running I'd be in trouble. Like, if I had my clothes off, I couldn't get to the fire escape. So I turned on the water a little bit and took off my shirt and washed with a washrag. Then I looked in a dresser and found some clean underwear and a clean shirt and put them on.

It took a long time, because I had to be so careful. By then I was really tired. I lay down on the bed to take a rest, and the next thing I knew it was morning.

Well, at least now I could see. There was the telephone next to the bed. I thought, Gee, I'd like to phone somebody. I could phone Mom. But what would I tell her? That I ran away? Or I could phone the Children's House and ask for Luke. They would say, Mr. Morehouse is not here any more. Then I'd laugh and hang up. Boy, would that surprise them!

But I figured the phone must be disconnected. Why would Mom pay the bill if she wasn't there? Just as I thought that, suddenly it rang. Boy, I must have jumped two feet in the air. It rang again. And again. I wanted to pick it up but I didn't dare. It rang about eight times and then stopped.

Who could be calling?

I thought, Well, I have to get out of here.

In the kitchen I found some cereal and a can of milk. I poured out the cereal and opened the can and started to eat. I found some crackers and a jar of jam. I had a real good breakfast. Then I went to put the milk in the refrigerator and I forgot myself. I slammed the door. I jumped away from the darn refrigerator and knocked a dish on the floor.

Then I waited. Sure enough, I heard footsteps. I grabbed my shoes and ran to the fire escape window and out. Just as I got out, I heard the door open and a voice saying, You see? Somebody was here.

I ran up to the roof just in time. I heard the

neighbor saying, See? They broke the window and got in.

I didn't wait. I ran across the roofs and down to the street. Then I made it to the subway.

It was about eight o'clock and people were going to work. That was good. The subway was crowded. Nobody would find me. I was on an express jammed with people. I couldn't have gotten off if I had wanted to. We'd get to a station and some more people would pack themselves in. I was in the middle of the car so I stayed there.

Then we came to a stop and they all started pouring out. I got pushed along with the mob, so I thought, Well, this is as good as anything. I went up the stairs and along a hall and there I was in the middle of the biggest building I ever saw. The roof was as high as the sky. It looked like the sky too, with stars painted on it. There were pictures too, people and animals, far away and hard to see. Nobody was looking at them but me. I saw a kid, he looked about teen-age, and I asked him, Hey, what is this place?

He said, What do you mean? It's Grand Central.

I said, Oh, yeah. I thought so but I wanted to be sure. I stood there watching the people carrying bags, going all different ways. Some were going through gates. I looked through a gate and saw that there were trains on the tracks.

I thought, So this is where the trains start from. Maybe some day I'll get on one and go someplace. Only not now. It takes money. I knew that much, that you couldn't just go under a turnstile like in the subway. And I knew something else, I would have to have some money pretty soon if I was going to eat.

I saw a woman walking with two heavy suitcases. She could hardly move. She'd put them down and rest. Then she'd look at the big clock and start again.

I went over to her and said, Want me to carry your bags?

She looked at me kind of surprised and scared, and started to say no. Then she changed her mind and said, Oh, all right. So I picked them both up, and were they heavy! I was surprised the woman could carry them at all. I went with her to the train and there was a man in a blue uniform. I got scared, thinking he was a cop, but he wasn't. He took the bags

and put them in the train. The woman gave
me two quarters.

She started to get on the train, and then she
stopped and said, Thanks for helping me.

I went back to the middle of the station and
looked for more people with too many bags. I
saw a woman with two kids and about six
shopping bags. She sure needed help but she
didn't look as if she could spare any money.

I got a few more jobs. One was a lady that
looked pretty rich—she had diamonds all over
her hands and her neck, anyhow they looked
like diamonds because they were shiny—and
she had me carry this bag out to a taxi, and
then she just got in the taxi and didn't give me
a cent.

But altogether I made about a dollar. By
then it was lunchtime and I bought myself a
couple of hot dogs and went and sat in this big
waiting room where there were a lot of people
on benches. Some had suitcases and were waiting for trains. But some were just sitting there,
like me. I was pretty tired by then. I was
wondering what to do next. I had to have
some place to stay. I was figuring maybe I
could sleep in the station somewhere.

Well, I was sitting there thinking and eating, and suddenly I noticed this kid on the bench near me, watching me eat. He looked about seven years old.

I said, Hi.

He didn't say a word but just watched me chew, as if he had never seen anybody eat before.

Finally I said to him, You want some? I held out my hot dog. He grabbed it and stuffed it in his mouth.

I said, Hey, watch it, you'll choke.

But he didn't choke. He swallowed it down and stared at me again.

I said, You want more?

He nodded. I said, Okay, come on, I'll get you one. Because I still had some money.

I got him a hot dog and a glass of milk. Then I bought some candy bars and we went back to the bench.

I said, What's your name?

He said, Ricardo.

I asked, Where do you live? What are you doing here? He shook his head again.

I was beginning to think he was stupid, when he started to cry. He didn't cry loud, just sniffled and wiped the tears away with his hand.

I asked him, Where's your mother?

He sniffled some more. I thought, Maybe he doesn't speak English. I said, Where your mama? (Any kid ought to know that word.)

He said, She go away. She go with man.

I asked him, What man? But he just shook his head.

I thought, This kid isn't all there. I better not get mixed up with him. And I got up to leave. But the kid got up too and came with me.

I said, Look, you go home. Maybe your mama is home already. I'm busy. And I walked away. But he came after me.

I said, Go on, get away from me. I'm not your brother. He put his arm up as if he was afraid I'd hit him.

I suddenly thought, He's scared to death, I can't leave him here.

He didn't look like a kid that could take care of himself. Some kids can. Like that Max. I bet even when he was six or seven he could grab enough to eat, or if not, he'd go up to some grownup and say, Mister, I'm hungry.

But this kid was scared out of his mind. I was getting scared too. This place was so big, it made me feel small as a cat. All the time I was running around doing things I was too busy to notice. But now I started to feel it. And if I felt small and alone, how did this kid feel?

I said, Okay, you can stay here with me awhile. Sit down. He sat down next to me. He leaned his head against me and after a while he got so heavy I looked at him and he was asleep.

I sat and watched the people. There were some old men sitting on benches doing nothing. There was a woman with a lot of shopping bags, and a man stretched out on a bench asleep. It looked as if those people lived there.

There was a woman behind a counter, selling papers and magazines, the one I bought the candy bars from. I thought of going over and saying, Lady, this kid is lost. Please take care of him. Then I'd get rid of him. But if I did that, she'd say, Who are you, what's your name and where do you live? And why aren't you in school?

I figured I'd have to take care of him myself. In a way it was better than being alone. But for that I'd have to have money. I woke him up. He jumped as if I had hit him.

I said, Look, Ricardo, I have to go someplace. You stay here and I'll come back soon.

But he grabbed me and said, No, no, don't
go!

I thought, Maybe that's what the kid's mother
said. So I told him, Okay, come with me. But
don't get in the way and don't hang on to me
like that.

We went toward the gates and I found a
couple more people who needed their bags
carried. One lady looked at Ricardo as if there
was something the matter with him, and another one asked, Why aren't you boys in school?

I said, We have double session, we're in
the first group so we get out early.

After I had a dollar, I said, Come on, Ricky,
we have to go in the men's room. You look too
dirty.

I took him in there and told him to wash his
face and hands. He didn't seem to understand
me. So I washed myself and said, Like this,
see, or you can't come with me. I don't want
no dirty kids around me.

Then I got some more food and then I started
worrying about where to sleep. Me, I figured
I could sleep anywhere. Maybe go back to the
park, or find an empty building. But I couldn't
drag the kid around with me.

I thought maybe we could find a place in the

station. I grabbed some newspapers out of a
trash can and we went looking for a place.
There were stairs, and tunnels, and hallways
and corners. If you haven't seen that place you
don't know how big it is. It would have been a
good place to play cops and robbers. Only not
just then.

Because suddenly the place started to fill up
with people. It was about five o'clock. People
were crowding in and running this way and
that. We got in the way and nearly got knocked
over.

I thought, if I wanted to, I could get lost in
the crowd and get rid of the kid that way.
He'd cry, and somebody would take care of
him. It was a good idea. Only—I couldn't do
it. I didn't figure out why till later. He trusted
me, that was why.

Of course I trusted people and they walked
out on me. So why should I care about this
stupid kid that I never saw before? Well, suppose Danny got lost. Wouldn't I want somebody to take care of him? Okay, so now I had
this kid to take care of.

But how could I?

The answer was, I couldn't. The best thing
was to take him to the Children's House, even
if it meant I'd get caught myself.

SIX

I said, Come on, Ricky, we're going someplace.

I put the papers in a can and we went to the subway. The kid didn't ask me where we were going. He just stuck close to me. There was a crowd on the platform, and he hung on to my shirt. We squeezed onto a train, jammed in among the people. It rattled and swayed along and at last it stopped at our station and we got off.

There was the park. It still looked green and nice. It was still spring, the same as when I walked there with the old man. It seemed like years ago. I looked to see if he was sitting on a bench, but he wasn't.

I said, Come on, and started up the street toward the Children's House. Up to that minute I hadn't really figured out what I was going to do. I knew I was going to take Ricky there, but I couldn't just dump him there and run. Anyhow, I didn't want to run. I was tired. I wanted somebody to take care of *me*.

So, as we walked up the street, I thought, Okay, I don't care what happens. Whatever it is, I'll have to take it.

We got to the building. I grabbed Ricky's hand and we walked up the steps. All of a sudden he was scared. He pulled back and said, No, I don't want to go. I pulled him, but he cried and hung back. Up to now he had done whatever I said, but something about the building scared him. He must have thought I was leaving him.

I said, Okay, if you don't want to go in, you can stay out. I'm going. And I walked up the steps and opened the door. So of course he came after me. We went inside.

It was suppertime. I could smell the food, and I could hear voices downstairs in the dining room. The hall was empty.

I thought, There must be somebody in the office. I didn't want to go in there. There's just something about an office that I don't like. But I had to do something about Ricky. So I went to the office and there was Mrs. Randal sitting at the telephone.

When she saw me, her mouth opened and she stared as if I was a ghost. Then she got up and came toward me and said, Julius! You came back!

Not, Where were you and what's the idea of walking out like that? But just, You came back.

I said, Yes, I had to. I found this kid Ricky. He's lost.

But she didn't pay any attention to Ricky, she just stared at me. Then she grabbed me by the arm and dragged me over to the telephone, and pushed a button, holding on to me as if she was afraid I would disappear. I heard her say, Julius is back.

Then things started happening. I heard feet running, and people calling, He's back? Who found him? What happened?

The place was full of noise and commotion.

Then I heard a voice saying, Julius! I looked, and there was Luke. He stood there looking at me over the kids' heads and then he grabbed me and I put my arms around him and put my head against him and cried. I couldn't help it. I tried to stop but I couldn't. Luke didn't mind. He just kept patting me on the back and saying, It's okay, it's okay, take it easy.

Then, just as I was getting hold of myself, there was a loud yell and somebody was grabbing me, hitting me, shouting, You went away! I don't like you! And all the time holding on to me and crying. It was Danny.

I looked at the kid and it was as if this was the first time I really saw him. I had gone away and left him, and he didn't know if I was ever coming back. I took hold of him and said, Cut it out, now. It's all right. I came back. Pretty soon he quieted down.

There was so much commotion that I forgot all about Ricky, when suddenly I looked around and there he was trying to sneak out the door. I ran and grabbed him and dragged him over to Luke.

I said, Here, take him. I came back because of this kid. He hasn't got any home, his mother left him in Grand Central Station. Somebody take care of him.

But Ricky wasn't having that. He was willing to go with me but not to be handed over to somebody else. He struggled to get away. I tried to hold him but he was too much for me. So finally Luke said, Look, everybody, let's calm down. Now Julius, we'll go into the living room and you explain things to him.

So we sat down and I said, Ricky, this is Luke. He's a real good guy. And this lady is Mrs. Randal, she's good too. And Ricky, this is Danny, my kid brother. You can be friends. Don't be scared.

Then Mrs. Randal got all the other kids to go back downstairs and finish their supper, and she brought some milk and sandwiches for me and Ricky, and for Danny too because he wouldn't go. I was hungry. I ate and drank.

Then I said to Luke, You came back.

He said, Mrs. Kronkite phoned me. She thought I might know where you went. So I got some time off to look for you.

I said, You did? Gee, I never thought of anything like that.

He told me, We went to your apartment and telephoned today and yesterday, and we put it on the radio. Several people thought they had seen you but when we got there you were gone.

I thought, Maybe that's why that kid brought his father—they heard it on the radio.

Mrs. Randal said, Julius, we were so worried. Your mother was so upset.

That made me feel real bad. I hadn't thought about her worrying. I only thought what would happen to me.

Mrs. Randal said, I phoned her just now so she would know you are safe. You can go and see her tomorrow.

I thought kids couldn't visit in hospitals, but she said they would make an exception this time.

I was waiting for somebody to start asking me questions. I was waiting to see if Max was there, and if he would say anything to me. Just then I saw him, standing in the doorway behind Luke, looking at me as if he was waiting to see what I would say.

I said, Hi, Max.

He didn't answer, just made a sign with his hand. I wasn't sure what it meant, and I didn't know what to do next. But Ricky took care of that one. He fell asleep with his head on the table.

Luke said, We better put him to bed. He picked him up to carry him upstairs, but Ricky woke up and began to yell. He wouldn't go without me, so we all went, Danny too.

Then Mrs. Randal wanted to give Ricky a bath and he yelled some more, so I said, Now listen, kid, Danny and I don't want to sleep next to any dirty kids, so you better get clean or you can't stay here. That settled it, only Danny had to take a bath too.

Well, at last they got to bed and they were both so tired they fell asleep right away.

I was pretty tired myself. I wanted to go to bed too and forget about everything, but I knew I couldn't. Maybe later, but not then. I had to do something else first. I went to look for Luke. He was sitting at the telephone in the office.

I didn't know how to begin. But Luke asked, Do you want to tell me anything?

I said, Yes. I did something bad. That's why I was afraid to come back. I thought the cops would be looking for me.

Luke asked, You did something bad enough for that?

I said, Well, it wasn't just me.

He asked me, Do you want to tell me who else?

I said, No.

He said, All right, what did you do?

So I told him, Well, there was this lady's pocketbook on top of her groceries, and this other guy took it and gave it to me, and I threw it away. There was no money in it, only stamps.

Luke said, Julius! *You* did that?

I said, Yes. The lady yelled, and a cop came, and I ran away. Then I was all alone, and I was hungry, so I took some food, and I asked people for money.

I told him everything that happened, and when I was finished he said, Well, Julius, I'm glad you told me. Do you feel better?

I said, Yes, a little. I wish I could give back the pocketbook.

He said, I know.

He didn't say anything else. He didn't have to. Maybe he knew the other guy was Max. He was a pretty smart man. I guessed that Max hadn't got arrested and hadn't told anything. But Luke didn't make me tell any more. I was glad about that.

Then I asked him, Luke, will you go with me to see my mother?

He said, Yes, I will, then I have to go back.

Well, that was like a slap. I forgot he only had a few days off. I said, Go back! What for?

Luke said, Look, Julius, get this through your head. I have a job. I'd rather stay here, but I promised to go back, so I have to go.

They believed me. Now you believe me too. I'll come to see you when I can. Okay?

I said, Okay.

So then he asked me, Well, will you promise to stay here and keep an eye on Danny, and on Ricky till they find his mother?

I promised. Only I didn't think they would find Ricky's mother.

Luke told me, Goodnight, you better get to bed now.

I was just going, when I remembered something. I felt in the pocket of my pants and said, Wait, Luke, I have to give you this.

I held out the magnifying glass. He took it and looked at it, and then he took my hand and put the glass in it and folded my fingers over it and said, Keep it, Julius, it's for you.

That all happened last spring. Luke went with me to see my mother the next day. I was scared to go. I didn't know if she had gotten worse from worrying about me, or if she would get excited and cry when she saw me. I didn't know if I should tell Danny I was going. But Luke said not to, he would want to go, and it would upset him to see her and then have to leave.

We went up to the hospital room and she was lying in bed looking much thinner than I remembered her. I went over and she grabbed me and hugged me and said, Oh, Julius, I'm so glad you're safe.

We talked awhile. She asked me why I ran away, and I said I didn't know, it was a dumb thing to do.

Luke said, I think Julius doesn't feel like talking about it too much. Later on he'll tell you. Is that right, Julius?

I said it was. Then I tried to tell her about other things, about Danny, and how I found Ricky, and she said, That was a good thing you did, bringing him to the Children's House.

I was glad she thought so.

She said, Well, I'll be home soon, and everything will be all right.

Pretty soon we had to leave. We went back to the House, and then it was time for Luke to leave. I hated to see him go. But I didn't say so, because he knew how I felt.

We shook hands and said good-bye, and I went inside.

Danny and I stayed at the House a couple of weeks longer. Then my mother went home so we could go too. We had to leave Ricky.

He didn't want us to leave, but we promised to come see him and let him come to our house sometimes.

On the way home I started thinking about the broken window. If Mama saw it before I had a chance to explain, she'd think somebody wanted to rob the place. Then she'd start worrying. But it was okay, the super fixed it.

Mama didn't go to work yet, but otherwise everything was back to normal. One day Luke came to see us on his day off. Gee, I was glad to see him. I asked him if he was going back to the House but he said no. He wanted to but he couldn't. It didn't make sense, because the kids needed him, and why couldn't that hospital get somebody else? But I guess not everything can make sense.

I still have the glass he gave me, and sometimes I look at things through it. It reminds me of Luke, and I remember that when I needed him most, he was there.